This Little Tiger book belongs to:

_____

_____

_____

_____

For Flora, Ron, and Elaine
~J. S.

For Glen P
~T. W.

LITTLE TIGER PRESS
An imprint of Magi Publications
1 The Coda Centre, 189 Munster Road, London SW6 6AW, UK
www.littletigerpress.com
First published in Great Britain 1996
by Little Tiger Press, London
This edition published 2008

ISBN 978-1-84506-889-9

Printed in China

3 5 7 9 10 8 6 4

I don't want to go to bed!

by Julie Sykes

illustrated by Tim Warnes

LITTLE TIGER PRESS

Little Tiger did not like going to bed.
Every night when Mommy Tiger said,
"Bedtime!"
Little Tiger would say,
"But I don't *want* to go to bed!"

Little Tiger wouldn't let Mommy Tiger clean his face
and paws, and he wouldn't listen to his bedtime story.
One night Mommy Tiger lost her temper.
When Little Tiger said, "I don't want to go to bed!"
Mommy Tiger roared, "ALL RIGHT THEN, YOU CAN
STAY UP ALL NIGHT!"

Little Tiger couldn't believe his good luck.
He scampered off into the jungle before
Mommy Tiger could change her mind.

Little Tiger went to visit his
best friend, Little Lion.
When he arrived,
Little Lion was having
his ears washed.

"It's bedtime," growled Daddy Lion.
"Why are you still up?"
"I don't want to go to bed!" said Little
Tiger, and he skipped off into
the jungle before Daddy Lion
could wash his ears, too!

Little Tiger decided to visit his second best friend,
Little Hippo.
He found him splashing in the river,
having a bedtime bath.

"It's bedtime," bellowed Daddy Hippo.
"Why are you still up?"
"I don't want to go to bed!" said Little Tiger,
and he scurried off into the jungle before
Daddy Hippo could give him a bath, too!

Little Elephant was Little Tiger's third best friend.

He went to visit him next.

Little Elephant was not out playing.

He was in bed, listening to his bedtime story.

"It's bedtime," trumpeted Mommy Elephant.

"Why are you still up?"

"I don't want to go to bed!" said Little Tiger,

and he bounced off into the jungle before

Mommy Elephant could put him to bed, too!

Little Tiger thought he
would go and find
Little Monkey,
his fourth best friend.
But he found Mommy
Monkey first. She put
a finger to her lips and
whispered, "Little
Monkey is fast asleep.
Why are you still up?"

"I don't want to go to bed!"
Little Tiger whispered back.
Quickly he tiptoed into the
jungle before Mommy Monkey
made him fall asleep, too!

Little Tiger didn't know where to go next. It was the
first time he had been in the jungle so late himself.
Even the sun had gone to bed!
Suddenly it seemed very dark.
What was that?

Little Tiger looked up
and saw . . .

. . . two very large yellow eyes
staring back at him!

The eyes belonged to a bush baby.
"Shouldn't you be in bed?" she asked.
"I don't want to go to bed,"
said Little Tiger
bravely. "*You* haven't!"
"That's because I go to
bed when the sun rises,"
said Bush Baby.

Little Tiger couldn't imagine going to bed in the sunshine! He shivered and thought how cold and dark it was in the jungle at night.

"I'm going to take you home," said Bush Baby.
"Your mommy will be worried about you."
"I don't want to go home! I don't want to go to bed!"
said Little Tiger. But he didn't want to be left alone
in the dark either.

So Little Tiger followed Bush Baby through the jungle.
He was glad of her big, bright eyes, showing him the
way back home.
"We're almost there," said Bush Baby, as Little Tiger's
steps became slower and slower.

"I don't want to go to . . ." said Little Tiger sleepily,
dragging his paws.
"Oh, there you are," said Mommy Tiger,
"just in time for bed!"

"I don't want to . . . " yawned Little Tiger,
and he fell fast asleep!
Mommy Tiger tucked him in
and turned to Bush Baby . . .

. . . but the den was empty.
Bush Baby had disappeared into
the jungle before Mommy Tiger
could tuck *her* in, too!

Fantastic reads from Little Tiger Press

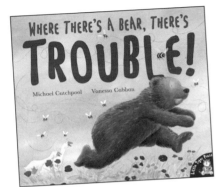

WHERE THERE'S A BEAR, THERE'S **TROUBLE!**

Michael Catchpool · Vanessa Cabban

You're Too Small!

Shen Roddie
Steve Lavis

BAA! MOO! WHAT WILL WE DO?

R.H. BENJAMIN
JANE CHAPMAN

I don't want to go to bed!

Julie Sykes · Tim Warnes

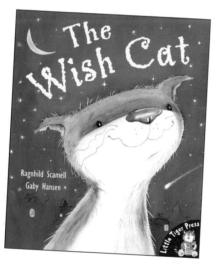

The **Wish Cat**

Ragnhild Scamell
Gaby Hansen

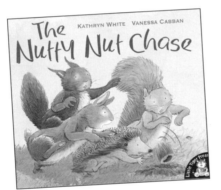

KATHRYN WHITE · VANESSA CABBAN

The **Nutty Nut Chase**

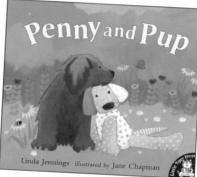

Penny and Pup

Linda Jennings illustrated by Jane Chapman

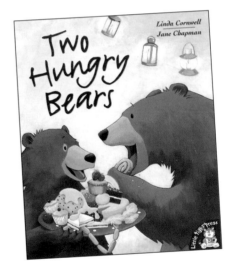

Linda Cornwell
Jane Chapman

Two Hungry Bears

THE GREAT GOAT CHASE

Tony Bonning   Sally Hobson

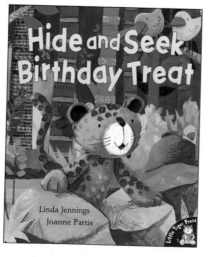

Hide and Seek Birthday Treat

Linda Jennings
Joanne Partis

For information regarding any of the above titles
or for our catalogue, please contact us:
Little Tiger Press, 1 The Coda Centre,
189 Munster Road, London SW6 6AW, UK
Tel: +44 (0)20 7385 6333 Fax: +44 (0)20 7385 7333
E-mail: info@littletiger.co.uk
www.littletigerpress.com